The Heavenly Host
Isaac Asimov

A Science Fiction Story

When young Jonathan Derodin arrives on Planet Anderson Two four days before Christmas, the leader of the earth settlement warns him to stay away from the Wheels, the planet's native inhabitants. They are dangerous creatures, he says, that want to kill humans. Yet when Jonathan accidentally meets one, he finds the little Wheel friendly and intelligent.

Then why does everyone believe they are deadly? And how can he convince the earth settlers that the Wheels are peaceful beings? Will he be able to stop the humans from destroying them all before it is too late?

How Jonathan and his new friend finally bring peace to Anderson Two during the season of good will makes a fast-paced, futuristic Christmas story.

The Heavenly Host

Isaac Asimov

Puffin Books

Penguin Books Ltd, Harmondsworth, Middlesex, England
Penguin Books, 625 Madison Avenue, New York, New York 10022, U.S.A.
Penguin Books Australia Ltd, Ringwood, Victoria, Australia
Penguin Books Canada Limited, 2801 John Street,
Markham, Ontario, Canada L3R 1B4
Penguin Books (N.Z.) Ltd, 182-190 Wairau Road,
Auckland 10, New Zealand

First published in the United States of America
by Walker and Company, 1975
Published in Puffin Books 1978
Copyright © Isaac Asimov, 1975
All rights reserved
A shorter and slightly different version of
The Heavenly Host was published in *Boys' Life*,
December 1974, under the title of "The Heavenly Host."

Library of Congress Cataloging in Publication Data
Asimov, Isaac, The heavenly host.
"A shorter and slightly different version...
was published in Boys' life, December 1974."
SUMMARY: Newly arrived on Planet Anderson Two just
before Christmas, Jonathan is warned about the dangerous
native inhabitants, but an accidental meeting with one of the
natives convinces him that they are friendly and peaceful.
[1. Science fiction. 2. Christmas stories] I. Title.
PZ7.A835He   1978   [Fic]   78-4553
ISBN 0 14 03.1117 3

Printed in the United States of America by
The Murray Printing Company, Westford, Massachusetts
Set in Highland

Dedicated to Andrea Horyczun

Contents

The Heavenly Host

1

The Little Wheel

Jonathan Derodin looked about the new planet curiously. It was named Anderson Two and it really was a new planet, at least for human beings. There was just a small area where humans lived and where the land had been made to turn green with Earth plants.

It looked as though he and his mother would be here for Christmas after all. There was no help for it. His mother was a planetary inspector. It was her job to decide whether certain planets were fit for human life or not. She had to go where her job called her.

They had been heading for Earth, which Jonathan had never seen, although he had read about it many times in his twelve years of life. His father, a mining engineer, was already there, and Jonathan and his mother were to follow.

Then the message reached them that she had to go to Anderson Two. Emergency, it said. Inspector Derodin had changed her plans at once.

"You can go on to Earth by yourself, Jonathan," she had said. "You're old enough to make the trip, and Christmas on Earth is really special."

Jonathan had been tempted, but the thought of an emergency on a brand-new planet, with his mother having to make important decisions, tempted him also.

"Would it be all right if I came with you, Mother?" he asked. "Or are you going to tell me there's danger?"

His mother smiled. "I don't think there's danger. And there'll be room for you on the space-cruiser that's coming to take me there. It's just that Christmas won't be quite the same on a young world like Anderson Two."

"That's all right," answered Jonathan. "I'll celebrate Christmas on Earth another time."

She was packing all the new smooth foam-fabric clothing she had bought for the vacation on Earth. Jonathan wondered if she was disappointed, too. If she was, she did not show it. Her face remained calm, and her brown hair was all in place. She acted as though it were a job she had to do and that was all there was to it.

When Jonathan was younger, she had once said, "You know, Jonathan, there was once a time when all human beings lived only on Earth. It was the only world with people on it. Now we're spreading out through hundreds and thousands of worlds, and someone has to decide whether certain worlds are fit for human beings or not. Such decisions are important."

Jonathan wondered why a world might not be fit for human beings, but he wasn't sure he ought to ask. It might be a foolish question, and he didn't want his mother to think he was foolish.

He was born on the planet Ceti Four, a planet that circled another Sun far from Earth. It seemed perfectly fine to him—friendly and homelike. It never had snow, though, and he sometimes wondered what snow was like. He had seen pictures of it on other worlds and on Earth. Scenes of Christmas on Earth always showed snow.

He wondered if there would be snow on Anderson Two. He read a folder on the planet as the space-cruiser took them there, and he decided there wouldn't be. At least not in the one place that human beings were living.

Once he was on the surface of Anderson Two, Jonathan was sure there wouldn't be. It felt warm and pleasant and it had to be cold for it to snow. He knew that.

He was curious about the new planet. He and his mother had arrived the day before, and all that time they had been in quarantine. They had to stay in a certain building away from everyone else while they were examined. This was to make sure they didn't bring dangerous germs to the planet. Now he was out of quarantine and he could wander about.

His mother had said, "Stay close to the Base, Jonathan, please." She said it absently, though. She was too busy to worry about him much. She was going into a conference with the leaders of the colony of the planet. She would have to see the Mayor, who seemed a short, cheerful man, and various councilmen.

Jonathan was glad he'd be left alone because he wanted to explore. The folder he had read said it was not a dangerous world. It certainly didn't seem so from what he could see.

He and his mother had been given a cabin near the spaceport. All the land around it looked very friendly and homelike. The houses were made of a kind of shiny rock that glittered a bit in the yellow sunlight (which seemed a little bit brighter than the sun back home at Ceti Four). Between the houses and all around them, it was green. There were grass and shrubs and, farther off, fields of grain on low, rolling hills. When he climbed to the top of one of them, he could see a river in the distance.

In the other direction, the green human world stopped. Jon took a road in that direction, and when it stopped, he found the land beyond was made up of rocky ridges.

Some of the rocks were lined with gray-brown crystals that made the edges sharp and glittery. He walked slowly out onto a ridge and stooped to look at the sharp edges more carefully. He put on his thin collagenite gloves and then, with a cautious finger, touched one of the rocks. The gloves protected his hands but did not interfere with the sensation of touch. He found that what looked like hard, brittle crystal was rather tough and rubbery.

He pinched along the edge and, with a little glassy sound, some of it broke off and fell. Jonathan snatched his hand away. He had not meant to do that. The folder had said that the crystals were like Earth plants. They absorbed carbon dioxide from the air and liberated oxygen just the way Earth plants did.

He saw that certain tan-colored rocks seemed to flow slowly until they reached the fallen crystals and covered them. He had read that those rocks were like earthly animals that live on the plants. Only they didn't have to eat plants for food. They could also absorb the energy they needed from the Sun.

He walked cautiously onward, trying not to jar any of the crystal edgings, or to step on any of the tan rocks. Once, when he did step on some of the rocks, they didn't seem changed in any way, and after that he walked more confidently.

He turned and could still see the patch of green human world clearly. He didn't want to get out of sight of that.

It was then that he saw his first Wheel, one of the native inhabitants of Anderson Two.

He didn't know it was a Wheel, of course, even though the folder had described them. What he saw was just a slab of rock about eight feet high, standing on its narrow edge in the sunlight, like a big figure 1. There didn't seem anything alive about it, but there was nothing else like it anywhere.

He was making up his mind to go closer and see what it was like, when from behind a rock there came another human being. He was looking at the big slab, too, looking so hard he didn't see Jonathan.

The man was inching forward slowly, and then his right arm started to rise and Jonathan saw that he had a blaster in it. It was then that it occurred to Jonathan that the slab must be one of the Wheels he had read about, and before he even thought about it, he was shouting, "Don't shoot it, mister!"

The man with the blaster whirled, his face twisting in surprise. He had a ruddy complexion and fiery red hair. He seemed so astonished at seeing Jonathan that for a moment he simply froze.

In that moment the slab of rock came to life. It

broke into a series of bright, flashing lights of various colors coming and going very rapidly. The top third and the bottom third of the slab each split into six parts. It seemed suddenly a large hand with six thick fingers at each end. The fingers spread wide, and then it went whirling away like a twelve-spoked wheel, turning end over end so rapidly that it blurred. Jonathan could see now why they were called Wheels.

The red-haired man turned back only in time to see the Wheel vanish. His hand was still tight about his blaster. He walked toward Jonathan with long strides, heedlessly cracking and breaking off the rock-crystal plants underfoot. Jonathan kept his eye on the blaster a little nervously. The man looked very angry.

The red-haired man called out, "Who are you? What are you doing here?"

Jonathan felt the urge to run, but he fought it down. There was no reason to run; he had done nothing wrong. He said, "I'm Jonathan Derodin. I'm just looking around."

The red-haired man's eyes narrowed. Some of the anger went out of his face. He looked cautious instead. "Are you with the Inspector?"

"She's my mother," said Jonathan.

"Why aren't you with her, then?"

"She's in conference, and I'm looking around. No one told me I couldn't."

"In conference?" The red-haired man suddenly turned and hurried off toward the patch of green that Jonathan could still make out.

Jonathan thought that perhaps he ought to go back to the Base, too. He wasn't sure what the red-haired man might say about what had happened. He turned to start going back, when his eye caught a movement. It was another Wheel, but a little one. It was not more than three feet high, with delicate spokes that turned slowly. It sparkled with lights, mostly in different shades of orange.

"I greet you."

Jonathan heard the words. But it was as though he had not really heard them, but thought them. They seemed to be in his mind at first, but then it was as if he had somehow heard them from outside. He looked about wildly. Was there another human being somewhere?

Then he looked at the little Wheel, and it sparkled in different oranges again and Jonathan heard "I greet you" once more. He heard it two more times and each time there were those sparkles on the little Wheel.

Jonathan asked, "Are you saying something to me, Little Wheel?" He felt foolish saying this.

But he heard, "Yes. When you make the funny noises I hear you in my mind. I heard you before when you were speaking to the Red-top."

Jonathan said, "When you make the funny colors, I hear you in my mind."

They came closer together, slowly, almost fearfully.

The little Wheel said, "Old Brown-Blue heard your noise. That's why he whirled. I heard you tell Red-top not to use his Exploder. You are a friend."

Jonathan said, "Was Brown-Blue the big Wheel that went away?"

"Yes. He can't hear the thoughts of you Sound-things. I can, though."

"You can?"

"Because I'm still little. I can hear your thoughts better than I can hear the others. Maybe because you're little."

"My name is Jonathan."

"I don't understand that," said the little Wheel.

"Jonathan," said Jonathan.

Slowly the little Wheel shone in spots of blue and purple, and Jon heard the sound inside his head, "Joneethin."

"That's pretty good," said Jonathan.

The little Wheel said, "My name is Yellger."

That was what the name sounded like in Jonathan's head, when one of the spokes of the little Wheel shone in two shades of yellow followed by a deep sea-green.

Jonathan said doubtfully, "Yellger?"

The little Wheel sparkled with rapid white flashes and there was the sound of laughter in Jonathan's head. "You say it very oddly," he heard, "but I understand."

They had gradually come closer to each other.

They were so close now they were almost touching. To Jonathan, this new way of talking was starting to seem like the most natural thing in the world.

2

Mother and Son

Pink had been hunting anxiously for some time now, careless of how she was using up energy. She even penetrated the shadows of the rocks, flashing brightly, and whirling slowly this way and that. Her twelve strong radiants moved easily over the broken ground.

Stupid Brown-Blue!

He had come back to the sunning-place with his

frightened tale of the Sound-things, those strange hateful creatures that never flashed but made sounds instead. One of them had tried to destroy him, Brown-Blue had said. The Sound-thing had had one of those things in his hand that exploded and destroyed.

"Why were you there?" one of the Wheels asked Brown-Blue. "Why were you so close to the green-place of the Sound-things? Didn't you know it was dangerous?"

Brown-Blue flashed confusingly. He managed to explain that he had been looking for the best-feeling sunlight and he had just wandered near the green-place without noticing. Then, at the last minute, he had become aware of the Sound-thing.

Pink had thrust herself forward, flashing, "How did you notice the Sound-thing? You never notice anything."

She was furious, and showed it in the deep violet edge to her flashes. By straying too closely to the green-place, Brown-Blue might have caused the

Sound-things to come out in groups and destroy every Wheel they could find.

Brown-Blue flashed, "I sensed a warning." His flashes were confused and dull. "I sensed a sound, and then I sensed the Red-top, and then I just whirled away as fast as I could."

His flashes reached out toward Pink and he said spitefully, "Yellger was with me. Maybe he's still there."

Pink looked about quickly. It had been hours since she had been aware of her young winged child. He was so small that he still had his wings. He was not in sight now, yet she refused to let herself be frightened.

"Why should he go with you, Brown-Blue?" she demanded. "What would he be doing with you?"

"You know your child best," said Brown-Blue. "You know how curious he is."

"Where were you standing when the Sound-thing came upon you?"

"I don't know," said Brown-Blue. "I had just been wandering." Then, as he began to feel guilty

18

over Pink's concern, his flashes took on a greenish tint. He said, "Maybe Yellger ran away, too."

Pink had to find her child now, and with the Sun sinking toward the horizon and its energy growing weak, she was seeking and flashing.

Had he been destroyed, or had he run away, as Brown-Blue had suggested? Even if he had run away that would not mean he was safe. He might have been trapped away from the sunlight. And if he was unable to soak up the energy from the Sun he might be starving.

Pink called him in little bursts of light. First there was a shade of golden yellow, then a deeper orange-yellow tint, and finally a rich jade green. Over and over, in the pattern of colors and spaces that she always used for him, she flashed, "Yellow-Yellow-Green — Yellow-Yellow-Green —" The colors came so rapidly that they slurred into "Yellger," which was what everyone called him. "Yellger," she flashed, over and over.

She didn't sense his call at first. Then she felt it, but it was far off—that distant glimmer of pink in just the shade Yellger had always used for her since he was newborn. "Mother!" he flashed, and then other flashes, "Mother, Mother, here I am!"

He was calling from the direction of the green-place of the Sound-things. She hurried toward the spot, whirling so fast that her radiants blurred and made her look like a great, rolling circle of stone.

His voice called, "Mother, Mother, it's all right," and for one moment Pink felt relieved. Then she saw, near him a *Sound-thing*. The Sound-thing was so close to Yellger that the two were nearly touching. It was smaller than those she usually saw, but size made no difference. It was the Exploders they carried that made them deadly and gave them the power to destroy whatever they wanted to destroy.

She could not see if the Sound-thing near Yellger carried an Exploder. She whirled forward faster than ever, trying to place herself between the Sound-thing and her child.

"Yellger! Little One! Whirl away! Whirl away!"

If only his wings were strong enough, he could have flown away, but it would be three days before the Wing-day arrived, when all the Little Ones of Yellger's group would have strong enough wings. On no account must Yellger risk injuring or straining those precious wings now. If he did, then he might not be able to join in the great time of flying.

Yellger did not move. "There is no reason to whirl, Mother," he flashed. "This is a friendly Sound-thing. I have sensed his sounds and I can make flashes out of them. He is called Joneethin."

Pink was not convinced. She faced the Sound-thing now. It was small in all its parts and its four limp radiants were motionless. She made a rush toward it and though she could see no Exploder in his grip, she half-expected to hear the terrible noise and to be destroyed. The Sound-thing moved away.

Yellger flashed anxiously, "Mother, do not drive him away."

Pink flashed, "You were in danger, Little One.

Come, come, I have told you so often to stay away from the green-place of the Sound-things. Now, when it is almost Wing-day, you disobey."

"But nothing happened, Mother."

"Nothing happened? Was he not ready to destroy that great fool, Brown-Blue?"

"Not *this* Sound-thing, Mother. It was the large Sound-thing, Red-top. My Sound-thing made noises to stop Red-top and Brown-Blue sensed the noise. That was why he ran. Joneethin *saved* him."

They had moved away now, far enough for Pink to feel safe. They were in a sunlit stretch where the sinking Sun could be felt in a dimming sweetness. Yellger unfurled his wings and let them vibrate in a faint hum.

Pink flashed, "Are you telling me, Little One, that the small Sound-thing could tele-flash? Do not tell stories."

"It is not a story. Little Ones can tele-flash. I could sense your flash long before I could see you, and you've told me over and over that you could tele-flash when you were young. Maybe little

Sound-things can tele-flash too. Only they tele-noise instead, because they make noises."

"Well, soak in the sunlight, Little One, and rest."

Pink's mind was busy. It was well-known that Little Ones could tele-flash, though some were better at it than others. Pink had been quite good at it when she was young and had her wings—but never as good as Yellger was. No one could sense flashes farther than he could. Was it possible that Yellger could even sense a Sound-thing's noises?

She flashed, "You couldn't sense the noises of a Sound-thing unless they were intelligent, unless they could think."

"But they are," flashed Yellger earnestly. "Joneethin could sense my flashes, too. He *is* intelligent—like us."

Pink murmured in a flash of very pale white. Was that indeed possible? To the Wheels it had always seemed that the Sound-things were un-thinking forces created only to destroy life. How could they be thinking beings and yet destroy?

It couldn't be, she decided. Yellger was imagining things. She flashed severely, "You might have been destroyed."

Yellger sparkled with laughter. "Joneethin had no Exploder. He said that he and his mother were going to a place beyond the stars, a place called Earth."

"A place called what?" Pink did not recognize that combination of shades of green and blue.

"He called it Earth. He is a friend."

"No, Little One. The Sound-things are not friends. They cannot be friends. They are changing our world. They are making it into a place of green fluttering things. They make more and more of the fluttering things each year. Perhaps some day all our pleasant world will be covered by fluttering green and the Sound-things will destroy us all."

"No, that won't happen, Mother. The Sound-thing is my friend. Sound-things can be friendly." Yellger stretched his wings outward to either side of his brown, chunky little body and let them grow pink. "Look, Mother, my wings are getting stronger. I showed them to the little Sound-thing. He doesn't have any."

24

"You should not have showed them, Little One. The Sound-thing might have hurt them."

"He admired them. He wished he had them. I told him about Wing-day and everything."

Pink sighed a tremulous, faint orange flash. Little Ones were always so eager for Wing-day. It would be wonderful, of course, for Yellger would then no longer be a child—but she wished he could stay a child just a little longer. She knew she was being selfish and she put the thought away. She flashed, "Only three more days now, Yellger. Then you will fly in the air with all the other Little Ones of your group. You will swoop and rise and hover and turn for many days. They will be wonderful days for you, Little One."

Yellger could detect the sadness in Pink's flashing, but he was busy thinking about flying and paid no attention. He flashed, "And then I will be grown up."

"No, Little One," flashed Pink, gently, "you will then only *start* growing up. All the sunlight energy that you will absorb through your wings will begin the changes. You will begin to grow larger and darker and stronger until you have Little Ones of your own. And *then* you will be grown up."

Yellger flashed, "But when the flying is all over, Mother, must I really lose my wings?"

"You really must, Little One. But do not fear; it will not hurt."

Both rested in the Sun.

Pink thought sadly, "Will my little Yellger grow up to have Little Ones, or will the Sound-things destroy us all?"

Yellger thought happily, "I hope Joneethin sees me when I'm flying."

3

Danger or Not?

Jonathan had not been afraid when he saw the large Wheel come whirling in. Yellger had told him, "That's my mother. She's worried about me, I guess."

Jonathan just moved away slowly, and said out loud, "I'm not doing any harm, Mrs. Wheel."

He heard Yellger say, "Mother, do not drive him away," and then the big Wheel stopped. Jon could not understand her flashes. He just heard confused sounds. It seemed as though messages went from mind to mind only in young people and young Wheels.

He turned to leave now and then he saw the man with red hair coming toward them in the distance—and his mother, too.

"You see him," the man said, "and you saw the Wheels."

Jonathan turned to look, but the Wheels were leaving rapidly.

The man with the red hair said, "Your son has no business here. He was in danger. Those Wheels are large and can kill."

Jonathan was running toward them now. He cried out, "There was no danger, Mother. The Wheels were doing no harm at all. This man tried to shoot one that was just standing there, doing nothing."

Inspector Derodin was calm. Her smooth hair, drawn backward, was completely unruffled and her dark eyes showed no anger. She held out an arm toward Jonathan and placed it on his shoulder.

She said, "I appreciate your concern, Councilman Caradoc, but Jonathan is a sensible boy and the reports I have on this world of Anderson Two stress that it is a calm world. It has an oxygen atmosphere, a terrain that is not dangerous, no large animal forms—"

"The Wheels are large," said Caradoc angrily. "You saw it for yourself. You saw it charging the boy."

"It was just trying to protect—" began Jonathan.

His mother's hand exerted just a bit of pressure on Jonathan's shoulder and Jonathan fell silent.

She said, "The Wheels are not exactly animals, since they feed directly on the energy of sunlight. That would almost make them plants."

"What difference does it make what you call them?" said Caradoc. "They are large and dangerous."

"It *does* make a difference," said the Inspector. "They do not eat living things; therefore they do not come equipped with claws or fangs and are not accustomed to killing. The reports say they are not dangerous."

Caradoc's lips twisted into a sneer. "The reports were written by people who came here for a while and left. I *live* on this world and I know better. You saw that Wheel charge."

"Mother," said Jonathan, urgently, but the pressure of her hand silenced him again.

Inspector Derodin said, "The reports say they have never harmed a human being."

Caradoc laughed. "They have not been given a chance to actually do harm. When they charge us, we blast them. It's self-defense. I myself have killed four in the last year and now they don't come near us. If your son comes out here and interferes with us when we try to protect him, I will not answer for the results."

And now the Inspector turned to her son. "What have you to say about this, Jonathan?"

"The Wheel was *not* trying to harm me, Mother."

Caradoc said, "It was charging you, boy. We saw that from the distance."

"She was his mother," Jonathan said, "the little Wheel's mother. She was just worried about Yellger—about her child. I backed away and she just went off with him. That's all."

"There *was* a smaller Wheel present, Councilman. I saw it," the Inspector added.

"What's that got to do with it?" asked Caradoc. "And what makes the boy think the big Wheel was the little one's mother? It's just a story he tells himself. We don't have to listen to that."

The Inspector said, "I don't think my son makes up stories. He is both intelligent and honest. Jonathan, what makes you say that the big Wheel is the mother of the little Wheel?"

Jonathan hesitated, then said, "Yellger told me so."

"Who's Yellger, Jonathan?"

"The little Wheel. That's his name."

Caradoc laughed.

Jonathan said angrily, "He *told* me so. Yellger told me so. That was what I heard when he made the light-flashes that are his name."

Caradoc shook his head and said, "Inspector Derodin, aren't we wasting our time? I don't want to say anything against your son, but I'm afraid he has a galloping imagination. These things are just rolling rocks. They don't have names except for those some youngster might make up for them."

"They are *not* just rolling rocks," said Jonathan, a little wildly. "Yellger talked to me all right. I understood him and he understood me. I told him about Earth and he told me about wings. He showed me his wings and said they were getting stronger and he would be flying soon, and I said Christmas was coming back on Earth and on other planets and maybe even here, and he said—"

Inspector Derodin interrupted her son. "All right, Jonathan." Turning to Caradoc, she said, "Now *that* at least is not my son's imagination. The Wheels do fly."

Caradoc said, "Yes, they do. But that's no secret. The report on Anderson Two mentions it and I'm sure your Colonization Board has it on file. You must have a copy on board the ship, since you keep telling me what the reports have to say about the planet. I suppose your boy must have read it."

"Did you read the report, Jonathan?" asked the Inspector.

"Yes, I did, but I didn't know it was secret."

"It wasn't secret and there was nothing wrong with reading it."

Caradoc said, "Nothing wrong at all, but that's where he got his information."

"That doesn't matter," Jonathan protested. "Even if I read something about wings, Yellger still told me. He showed me his."

Caradoc looked annoyed, but then he managed to smile and say, "Well, I won't argue with the boy. Just the same, it is not right for him to break the rules governing behavior on this planet. Our young people are not allowed to pass beyond the boundaries of the green plant life, and they do not do so. Your son set a bad example and it was dangerous besides. I don't think it should happen again."

The Inspector's cheeks flushed a little, but she

said evenly, "Jonathan was not aware of the rule. He was not told. Naturally, he will not do it again. Shall we go back to the council-room now and continue our discussion?"

She walked slowly back toward the green Base with her arm still on Jonathan's shoulder. She said, "Anderson Two seems an interesting planet."

Caradoc nodded. "The soil will grow anything and it could be made into a paradise. The trouble is that we can't attract immigrants as long as we don't have a final classification as a Human World. No one wants to start making a home for themselves if there's a possibility they'll have to leave. If we don't get the classification soon, the colony will fail."

"Yes," said Inspector Derodin, "I quite understand why you should be anxious. Your Mayor has explained the situation to the Colonization Board and they sent me here on an emergency call. You see we understand your situation."

"May we have the necessary classification, then?"

"Ah, but there is some question as to the presence

of native intelligent life here on Anderson Two. You surely understand that the basic rule by which we are colonizing the stars of the Galaxy is that we must never settle ourselves on a world that already has an intelligent life-form. We would wish to be treated the same if some other intelligence tried to colonize one of our worlds."

Caradoc said, "There is no intelligent life-form on this world except for human beings."

"Might not the Wheels be intelligent?"

"Because your son claims he has talked to them?" Caradoc's voice became angry and his face grew almost as red as his hair.

"No, no. There are some reports that the Wheels *do* communicate. They flash lights in varying colors and at varying intervals."

"So do fireflies on Earth," said Caradoc.

"Not in nearly so complicated a fashion. The flashing *could* be a communication device. If so, they may be intelligent. This planet must then be left to them."

"I've heard this before," said Caradoc, impatiently. "For years now, someone mentions this every once in a while. But no one has ever proved it. No one has ever shown that the flashing lights are really a communications device. How long must this world wait?"

"Well, there's something to that," said the Inspector, pleasantly, "but let us have a few days to think about it. It will soon be Christmas and there's no reason we can't wait till after the season. After all, I understand you've had a large Christmas tree shipped in from Earth, so why not forget business for just a little while and try to substitute a little old-fashioned Christmas spirit?"

Caradoc shook his head. "There's no reason you can't give us an answer right now and *then* celebrate Christmas. Then we'll really have something to celebrate."

"We might find ourselves celebrating a hasty decision we would all regret. No, Councilman, give me three days, and then you will have my decision."

They were back on the green grass of the Base again.

Jonathan accompanied them silently. He was very upset. He didn't like that red-headed Caradoc, and he didn't like the way he was trying to rush his mother into giving him her answer.

Jonathan knew enough about his mother's work to understand that once a planet became a Human World, its whole life-system was changed to an Earth-type so that human beings could live on it comfortably. If Anderson Two was established as a Human World, all its land would be planted with trees, grass, grain, and all its sea would be filled with fish. Millions of people would come to live on the world and Councilman Caradoc would be one of their leaders. He would rule a world.

And on a Human World all the native life, except for some of it kept in special parks for scientific study, would be killed. All the Wheels would be killed.

If the Wheels were intelligent, though, the planet could not be made into a Human World. The human beings already on it would have to leave and Caradoc would have to go somewhere else where he would just be an ordinary person.

Naturally, Caradoc wouldn't want anyone to think the Wheels were intelligent, and he would say that Jonathan's tale of talking to the Little Wheel was just a boy's imagination. How could Jonathan prove this was not so? How could he make it clear to everybody, to *everybody,* that the Wheels were intelligent?

Jonathan was not supposed to leave the Base. He knew that. Caradoc had said so, and his mother had said so. But he had to. He had to save the Wheels somehow and that was more important than what might happen to him if they caught him.

Fifteen minutes after he had been taken to the cabin and left there, he was out again and walking quickly over the grass to the brown rocky region beyond.

4

The Wings

Yellger was looking for Jonathan, too. It made him happy to talk to a Sound-thing. Jonathan's thoughts were different and his tales about the way Sound-things lived were odd and interesting.

Of course, Pink had told him not to do this, but Yellger felt he must. Carefully, he moved closer to the green area, keeping watch for large and dangerous Sound-things. He flashed the green-signals that were Jonathan's name and tried to think very hard as he did so, in order to drive the thought as far as possible.

Almost at once, he felt Jonathan's thoughts in return and could just faintly hear a distant sound. Yes, thinking hard *did* send the thoughts farther.

But then he stopped. There was a feeling of danger about Jonathan's thoughts, a feeling of death for the Wheels. Yellger began to flicker uncertainly. Surely Jonathan did not want to destroy the—*no*, it was danger to the Wheels from others, from Red-top.

Yellger moved quickly toward the place from which Jonathan's thoughts were coming. He flashed, "I am glad to see you again, Joneethin, though I should not be here."

"I should not be here either," said Jonathan. "But I must talk to you. Tell me about Wing-day. Tell me when it will be. You said it would be soon. *How* soon? *How* soon?"

The thought seemed very anxious and Yellger was pleased to flash the explanation. He was looking forward to it with such delight that he wanted to share it with his new Sound-thing friend. Yellger explained that the Little Ones grew slowly till their bodies were almost ready to be grown up and needed only a great flood of sunlight energy to set off the change. The wings grew while they were little until those wings were strong and ready. Then came the glorious days when the Little Ones flew and flew and flew day after day. They flew while their outspread wings took energy from the Sun, until enough had been absorbed. Then the Little Ones would sink down to the ground. Their wings would wither and fall off and they would never fly again.

"Do you flap your wings?" asked Jonathan.

"I do not understand the thought. What we do is this. See?"

Yellger unfurled his delicate wings from their curled position against his body—a curled position in which they were scarcely noticeable. For a while, they shimmered like large, fuzzy, gently curved feathers of the purest white. Then they vibrated and Yellger lifted a tiny bit off the ground.

He came down again and flashed, "I must not use them now. They will not be ready for flying for three days."

Jonathan's thoughts seemed slow and deep. He said, "Are there many of you Little Ones, Yellger?"

"In our tribe there are many dozens of my group waiting for Wing-day."

For a while, Jonathan made no sounds and his thoughts were just a faint murmur. Then he said, "In three days it will be Christmas."

"I do not understand the thought," said Yellger.

It was Jonathan's turn to explain now, and he did so for a long time.

Yellger interrupted once or twice to say, "I do not understand," and Jonathan's thoughts grew more urgent than ever.

It was nearly the end of day when Jonathan lifted his head and suddenly called out, "Yellger! Away! Quickly!"

There was no need for the warning for Yellger

had heard the coming of the other Sound-things even before Jonathan had. Yellger was whirling away quickly, when the sound of the Exploder came.

5

Waiting

Jonathan's mother was angry and it sounded in her voice. "You've broken the rules, Jonathan, and you deliberately disobeyed me. Councilman Caradoc has every right to punish you for this and it would be wrong of me to stop him from doing so."

"But, Mother, I *had* to go back. The Wheels are intelligent."

Inspector Derodin shook her head. "There's no real evidence for that. I know that you say you talk to them, and I'm sure you think you do, but it's not enough, Jonathan. The things you say they tell you you might have found out in other ways. *I* know you are not a liar, but the others don't."

"What if I find out something I couldn't find out any other way?"

"Such as?"

"The folder I read—the report, you know—said there were times when the little Wheels flew, but it didn't say when. I know exactly when because Yellger told me. It's three days from now, on Christmas. You'll see."

Inspector Derodin said thoughtfully, "You're right, Jonathan. Wing-day changes from year to year because the year of Anderson Two is a little longer than the year on Earth. This year Wing-day *will* come on Christmas. How did you say you found out?"

"Yellger told me."

The Inspector sighed. "It's not convincing enough, Jonathan. They'll say that someone here at the Base told you."

"But that's not so. You know it's not so, if I tell you that."

"My believing won't help."

"Yes, it will, Mother. You're the Inspector and if you decide not to certify this planet as a Human World, that's it. So don't certify it."

"I can't do that without a cause, Jonathan. You know better than that. I must have a good reason."

"The Wheels are intelligent."

"I must have proof. I'm sorry, Jonathan, but your word simply isn't strong enough. You communicate with the Wheels by telepathy, but you're the only one who does. If there were only someone else, too."

"You have to be young to communicate, Yellger says. He and I are both young."

"Jonathan, there are young people on Anderson Two, many of them younger than you are. None of them have exchanged thoughts with the Wheels."

"None of them are allowed to go near the Wheels, that's why. That old Caradoc said that none of the kids are allowed to get off the Base and explore the parts where the Wheels are. I'll bet they're not allowed to go there just so they won't be able to communicate with the Wheels."

"That may be so," sighed Jonathan's mother, "but we can't prove that."

"It's so just the same," said Jonathan. "I'm sure it is. In fact, some of the kids here probably *did* exchange thoughts with little Wheels. Maybe they said so and that's why that Caradoc guy is so anxious to have you sign the papers. He's got to have the right to kill off all the Wheels before anyone finds out they're intelligent."

Jonathan's mother looked more thoughtful than ever. "I wish I could believe you, Jonathan, but there's no evidence. After all, Councilman Caradoc might just be anxious to make this world a true home. After all, that's a reasonable desire."

"That can't be all he wants. I *know* the Wheels are intelligent. I can prove it if—if—"

"If what?"

But Jonathan shook his head. "I don't know. I tried to explain to the little Wheel about Christmas, but I don't know if he understood me. And they shot at him while he was whirling away and I'm not even sure he got away safely. If he's all right, and if he understood, then maybe—"

Jonathan felt terrible. He wasn't at all sure Yellger had understood or that he could explain it to the other Wheels, or that he was even alive.

He said, "Mother, could you stall them for a while and not give them their colonization papers until I can think of something else?"

Inspector Derodin shook her head. "I don't think that can be done, Jonathan. This world has been waiting for a long time and I said I would make my decision after Christmas came. It would be a Christmas present for this world, and I can't deny it to them. If there is no real evidence that the Wheels are intelligent by then, I will have to grant their request."

Jonathan shook his head. He had never in his life felt so unhappy.

6

The Little Wings Fly

It was as busy and happy a time on Anderson Two this Christmas as it would have been on any other Human World where Christmas was celebrated.

For the first time, Jonathan saw the kids who had been born on Anderson Two and who lived there. In the mild weather of the little town, they sang carols in the streets and helped decorate the large tree that stood right in the middle of the main street intersection. The Base was so small that presents in gaily colored packages could be piled up under the tree for everyone in town.

For a little while, Jonathan felt guilty about trying to get human beings off Anderson Two. All these kids belonged here. It was their home. Why should they be driven away? But then he thought that, after all, there were thousands of Human Worlds that would take in all these people and make them comfortable, but Anderson Two was the only world the Wheels had.

A small spaceship had landed at the port earlier in the day. It had come to lift Inspector Derodin and Jonathan off Anderson Two and transfer them to a large liner that would carry them to Earth.

The Mayor greeted the dozen men and women of the spacecrew and said, "You are in time to celebrate Christmas with us."

Councilman Caradoc added, "Yes, and it's a double celebration, because the Inspector will sign the colonization papers at the end of the festivities."

He seemed in a very good humor and Jonathan was sure he knew why. Seeing the spaceship, Caradoc felt that the Inspector and Jonathan would soon be leaving his world. He wanted them off so that he could go on destroying the Wheels with no one to stop him.

All through the day, Jonathan had peered up into the sky, hoping and hoping. Sometimes he thought he saw a little Wheel very high in the air, beginning the flights of Wing-day. But what he saw were just tiny bright specks, and he couldn't tell if they were the Wheels.

If one of them was Yellger, Jonathan might hear the thoughts coming from him—or from another Little One. But though he concentrated his mind as hard as he could, Jonathan could sense no thoughts. More and more he began to feel that Yellger was dead, that he had been killed by the blaster that had been fired at him as he was whirling away.

The dinner was over at last. Santa Claus landed from a sleigh that moved through the air on force beams, and he handed out toys to the younger children. The services were completed, and everyone but Jonathan was happy.

Caradoc said, "Mr. Mayor, I think this might be a good time for the Inspector to sign the papers."

Inspector Derodin looked toward Jonathan, who moved his lips to say, "Don't," without making any sound.

Inspector Derodin hesitated, then said, "Yes, I will sign them."

The Mayor placed the colonization forms on the table and Caradoc said, "I think the men and women of the spaceship should move closer and witness the signature. It would be useful to have human beings from other planets see the moment when Anderson Two becomes a Human World."

Inspector Derodin lifted her specially coded pen, and had just placed it on the line marked off for signature when a rising babble of voices stopped her. She looked up.

Jonathan cried out, "It's the flying Wheels!"

He was waving his arms and pointing. They had

not killed the little Wheel after all. And Yellger *had* understood and remembered.

They were swirling dots in the sky at first, brilliant white dots, giving off some of the energy of sunlight that they had absorbed all day long. Jonathan tried to count—twenty—thirty—there were at least fifty.

They were almost overhead now. They sank in a cluster—lower—lower—

Every man, woman, and child was looking upward.

They came still lower. The flying Wheels were pure white, every one of them. All had their wings extended, and the soft hum of their quivering could be heard. Finally, someone said, "They look like angels!"

The Wheels were moving, adjusting, placing themselves in position. Then they all came to a halt, hovering in the air a hundred feet above the Christmas tree in a formation that made them a glowing, shining, white five-pointed star—a living Star of Bethlehem.

Inspector Derodin caught her breath at last and said firmly, "These are intelligent beings, Councilman Caradoc. You can all see that now. *You* see it, Mr. Mayor, don't you? So do you men and women of the spaceship crew. This world can *not* be colonized."

She tore the colonization form in two, then four, then eight pieces, without ever removing her eyes from the star formed by the hovering, winged Wheels.

"Wait," said Caradoc, "you can't deny us. Your boy told them what to do."

Jonathan cried out, "Sure I did. But how could I tell them anything, and how could they understand anything, unless they were intelligent?"

Caradoc's mouth moved, but he was silent.

Inspector Derodin, still watching, said softly, "And suddenly there was with the angel a multitude of the heavenly host praising God, and saying, 'Glory to God in the highest, and on earth peace, good will toward men.'"

Jonathan had never been happier. Yellger and

his friends would be safe. This planet would be left to the Wheels. "In the universe peace, good will toward all intelligent beings," he whispered.